The Disgusting Sandwich

By Gareth Edwards

Illustrated by Hannah Shaw

ALISON GREEN BOOKS

Rumble...
Rumble...

WELCOME

In a clump of trees on the edge of a park there lived a badger. He was a very hungry badger, and his tummy wouldn't stop rumbling.

One day a boy came to the park.
He had a sandwich with him.
It had fresh white bread
and peanut butter.

It was a

beautiful

sandwich.

The boy took his sandwich to the playground.

He was about to take a bite when a girl bumped him and it fell in the sandpit.

Now the fresh white bread was
covered in gritty sand.

"Well," said the little girl,
"you can't eat it now.
It's disgusting."

A squirrel found the sandwich.
She didn't mind the sand.

She carried the sandwich into a tree
to share with her children.

But they weren't good at sharing . . .

. . . and the sandwich dropped out of the tree . . .

. . . and into a pond.
"Well," said the mother squirrel,
"we can't eat it now.

It's disgusting."

A frog saw the sandwich. It was floating in some goopy green pondweed that smelled of rotten eggs. The frog didn't mind the sand, and the smelly green goop. He pulled the sandwich out to eat it on the path.

But a boy on a scooter raced by
and he had to jump out of the way.

Now the sandwich had big black
squish marks right across the middle.
"Well," said the frog, "I can't eat it now.
It's disgusting."

Next a crow saw
the sandwich.

She didn't mind the sand,
the smelly green goop
and the big black
squish marks.

She peeled the sandwich off the path
and flew proudly up to her nest
to give it to her mum.

But a scary flying thing frightened her
and she dropped the sandwich into an ants' nest.
Hundreds of ants crawled all over it.

"Well," said the crow's mum,
"I can't eat it now.
It's disgusting."

Soon a fox found the sandwich.

He didn't mind the sand, the smelly green goop, the big black squish marks or the hundreds of ants. He took it to be a present for a lady fox he liked.

But when he opened his mouth to tell her how nice she looked
the sandwich fell into a pile of feathers that had somehow got there.

Now the sandwich was covered with grimy old feathers.
"Well," said the fox's friend, "I can't eat it now. It's disgusting."

And she kicked the sandwich
into a flower bed . . .

. . . and went off to go
through some bins.

CLANG!

In amongst the flowers were
some slugs. They didn't mind the sand,
the smelly green goop, the big black squish marks,
the hundreds of ants or the grimy old feathers. They
slithered all over the sandwich and criss-crossed it with
trails of slippery slime and oozy grey bubbles.

The moon came out.

Finally, along came the badger.
He was hungrier than ever.

He gazed at the sandwich, all covered in sand
and smelly green goop and big black squish marks and
hundreds of ants and grimy old feathers and slippery
slime and oozy grey bubbles glistening
in the moonlight.

His tummy rumbled.

Rumble...
Rumble

So he ate
up all the
slugs.

But he didn't eat the sandwich.
It was too disgusting.

For Joseph, Imogen, Hester and Kit,
my children, who can spot a badger
with potential – G.E.

For Ben, heroic slug rescuer and
fan of disgusting sandwiches;
& Alison, Zoë and Rebecca,
the wonder team! – H.S.

First published in the UK in 2013 by
Alison Green Books
An imprint of Scholastic Children's Books
Euston House, 24 Eversholt Street
London NW1 1DB, UK
A division of Scholastic Ltd
www.scholastic.co.uk
London – New York – Toronto – Sydney – Auckland
Mexico City – New Delhi – Hong Kong

This edition first published in 2015, exclusively for Scottish Book Trust

Text copyright © 2013 Gareth Edwards
Illustrations copyright © 2013 Hannah Shaw

ISBN: 978 1 407165 35 6